Read what reviewers said about "I Am Me:"

"These teens are the voice of a generation that, if allowed to speak loud enough, might pave the way for change. As a psychotherapist working with adolescents, self-esteem, and eating disorders, and as a parent, I hope this book sells millions, both to benefit individual teens and our society as a whole."
Lisa M. Schab, L.C.S.W., Psychotherapist and author

"This book is a beautiful anthology of heartfelt poetry and art by teens. Reading this collection will help teens feel connected and know they are not alone."
Heather Hinds, School Psychologist

"Utterly stunning. If I told you it was just artwork and poems it would be a diservice to this amazing collection of work. The artwork by teens is so good it restores your faith in the arts. The poems are also excellent.... Absolutely worth having for your teen."
Joshua Cartwright, Librarian

"Edgy...the writing and artwork really reflect some of the things I wrestled with as a teen."
Massie Bergeron, Teacher, Ferrucci Jr. High School, WA

"Powerful, insightful and honest. The art and poetry are the perfect way to express strong feelings and introspective thoughts."
Cathy Overman, Teacher, Schuylkill Valley High School, PA

"Lots of heart and soul throughout the pages."
Cherri Stephenson, Teacher, North Harrison Middle School, IN

"This book will help our school counselors as they deal with students' image problems."
Jan Renard, Teacher, Monte Vista Christian School, CA

"Every page is powerful and sends a poignant message."
Lisa Lorch, Teacher, Inter-Lakes Middle Tier School, NH

"Not only did this book lead to productive discussions about societal pressure, it also inspired my students to express their personal feelings and thoughts more openly."
Chelsey Funk, Teacher, Kennewick High School, WA

"Between the artwork and the poetry, the message is nothing short of powerful. As an adult, many of the poems spoke to me and would definitely speak volumes to my students."
Brianna Walter, Teacher, Mt. Pleasant-Blythedale Union Free School District, NY

I AM ME

Teen Artists and Writers
Speak Out on Being Yourself

Edited by Tom Worthen, Ph.D.

Published in a collaborative effort by:

S

I AM ME
Teen Artists and Writers
Speak Out on Being Yourself

Authors and artists are responsible for the originality of the work submitted.

CREATIVE COMMUNICATION
PO BOX 303 · SMITHFIELD, UTAH 84335 · TEL. 435-713-4411
WWW.POETICPOWER.COM · WWW.CELEBRATINGART.COM

ISBN: 978-1-60050-807-3

Cover art by Kaylie Spencer, Grade 11

Foreward

The poems, essays and art in this collection were gathered from writing and art contests sponsored by Creative Communication and Celebrating Art. For the past twenty years, we have published thousands of students and given them the opportunity to be published and be recognized in areas that often go unnoticed.

The idea for this book came from several places. First, as editor at Creative Communication, I listened to the voices that emerged from students who wrote about the feelings of finding themselves. These voices talked about being alone, lost and trying to fit in. Second, as editor at Celebrating Art, I saw pieces of art that were rendered beautifully, but did not have an audience beyond our original contest. These pieces give an important visual representation to the writing. Finally, as a professor in Interpersonal Communication, I read the research on youth that often lose themselves trying to conform to peers and society. I wanted to create a book to let these youth know that they are not alone.

The pressure of conforming and the realization that you don't have to acheive "perfection" to be "perfect" is not isolated to a specific sex, orientation or gender. As you view these images and read the writing associated with them, I hope you relate to some, if not all the pieces selected. If you leave this book with the feeling that you are not alone and it is okay to be yourself, then this project was a success.

Tom Worthen, Ph.D.
Editor – Creative Communication and Celebrating Art

**To be considered for future collections of art and poetry,
enter your work at:**

WWW.POETICPOWER.COM (Grades K-9)

WWW.CELEBRATINGART.COM (Grades K-12)

I AM ME

Teen Artists and Writers Speak Out on Being Yourself

Acceptance

In this world we live in,
Everyone wants to be accepted.
No one wants to have that feeling,
That pain of being rejected.

We all want to be that somebody,
And we try to conform.
We kill that person inside of us,
Leaving our spirit unborn.

Be yourself — do not change,
Uniqueness will keep you strong.
Because acting and being fake,
Is just plain wrong.

Sara Werwie, Grade 11

Art by Sayoko Ariga, Grade 12

Perfect Girls

We are the grey, the undefined, the perfect.
You see our exteriors
Painted on with brushes, covering every blemish
Sparkling our eyes with powder
To make them,
Pop.

Our smiles plastered, beaming eye to eye,
If you will look closely, dear, you will see
They don't quite reach

For we are Splenda fake,
Sweet and sugary with
Zero calorie count.

We are the many, the every, the perfect.
We are breaking down slowly
Inside,

Inside,
You do not see our cracks,
Caving in.
You do not see our imperfections,
Our secrets,
Our hidden desires
For we are the perfect girls.

Sara Bradley-Bussell, Grade 12

Art by Deanna Nguyen, Grade12

Perfection

Perfection, what everyone seems to aim for.
You have to aim for it to be "normal."
Why can't people see we are all different?
We all can't fit into a certain mold —
We don't all believe the same things,
Each perspective is different.

Perfection is overrated,
It causes you to change everything.
It can rip you apart.
So tell me — who invented this thing called "perfect."

Doesn't it seem like everyone wants you to fit in a mold.
Parents, teachers, peers, and friends.
They all want you to be perfect.
If you step out of the box,
    or believe something different you're "crazy."
When you mess up, you get unnecessary punishment.

Why can't society accept us for who we are?
Different! A unique person!
We all have special qualities,
I want mine to shine, not put into the mold called perfection.

Maranda Bowling, Grade 10

Art by Angell Hammersmith, Grade 9

Perfection

Plastic
The substance is melted into the pores of humanity
They hide behind the mask of glass and the smell of paint

The dollies don't like the real boys and girls
They do not fit the cookie cutter standard of beauty

Barbies tend to laugh at the all-American dolls of society,
    for they look too real
Real is ugly
The right nose, but wrong foot size,
      causes you to be kicked from
      the pretty pink home of lies

You don't have to be perfect to be seen
      as pretty in the eyes of the right beholder

Your nose, feet, stomach, and everything in between
is absolutely beautiful
You are special and unique
You are perfect

Courtney Ekstrom, Grade 10

Art by Lindsay Frank, Grade 12

ASHION
MAKEUP
WHY?
ake fit happen.
E LOOK
High Anxiety.
Discreet
QUIET,
Mask
CULTURE
ERO
MISTAKES.
Made you look.
ALONE.
Value
Reduce the look
WHAT WOULD YOU DO
BEAU
BECAUSE THEY'RE DOING IT
OUT-OF-THE-WAY

A Beautiful Person

beauty begins
the moment you decide
you need to be yourself
it doesn't take gallons of foundation
to make your face beautiful
or the best makeup on the planet
think of it as a flower
a flower does not compete
to the one next to it
for it just blooms
beauty is about individuality
because
being you
is the best person you can be
there is no reason
to hide
who you truly are inside
and know
never apologize for being yourself
you were born to be real
not perfect

Meranda Schmaltz, Grade 11

Art by Breanna Bui, Grade 11

The Eye of the Beholder

I'm not perfect
And that's just me
Me is all I could ever be.
I'm not skinny
And I'm not tall.
That's just not how I was made
That's all.
I don't have long hair
And my eyes aren't green or blue.
But I wasn't made to be just like you.
When will people realize
That we weren't all made the same?
It's not our fault we're different
We all have God to blame.
I know I'm not perfect.
I know I'll never be.
So why don't you just be you.
So I can just be me.

Natalie Sherrell, Grade 10

Art by Alexander Durrence, Grade 11

Imperfection

I am not perfect,
Nor have I ever claimed to be,
All that I ask is that when looking in the mirror,
I can see a perfectly imperfect me.
I am no girl from the front of a magazine cover,
Or a model tall and thin,
I am me, just me, learning to be comfortable in my own skin.
Be proud of who you are,
As God made you unique,
Stand tall, proud, and with your head held high,
You'll find it's your best technique.
So love yourself for all things you,
And learn from your mistakes,
But never doubt for a single second,
That being a perfectly imperfect you is at stake.

Madison Barkley, Grade 11

Art by Emily Cai, Grade 12

What Does Imperfection Mean?

If a single fault stops anyone from going after their dreams then nobody in this world would accomplish anything because nobody is flawless. Flaws make each person special. Surely, our flaws can work against us, but they can also work for us, it all depends on our beliefs. Confidence is essential, but imperfections should never define our level of self-image or self-worth. In fact, looks are not always a guide to one's true character.

As long as you focus on what truly matters and on actions that shape integrity, you can be successful and enjoy life, no matter what. Today, let us embrace our flaws and stop living in an "I must be perfect" bubble.

Remember flaws make each individual unique and imperfections never define a person. Therefore you must ask yourself now: What does it mean to look into the eyes of imperfection?

Herminia Chow, Grade 9

Art by Isabeta Rountree, Grade 10

What Lies Beneath

Each and every day
She applies a mask
To hide who she really is
But all the makeup in the world
Can't cover all of her pain
All of her sorrow
And all those name brands
Cannot conceal it.
They're just disguises
So in society she can be almost
"Perfect."
But behind all that foundation, eyeliner
And mascara there is a beautiful girl
And maybe, just maybe, one day
She can remove her disguise,
Go out into the world
And show society what perfect looks like

Jillian Spreckels, Grade 10

Art By Raelle D'Altilio, Grade 12

Perfection

The mirror I stand before, show my flaws I try to ignore.
The marks on my arm show all the pain I've bore.
The tears in my eyes, show my world is falling,
and my silence is the sound of me crying.
My biggest fear is that you'll see me the way I see myself,
and hear my smile…calling for help.
My lips are sealed, eyes are closed,
ready for my fate I already know.
But the whispers keep laughing and make fun of me.
And my flaws come to the surface, for all to see.
But it doesn't matter for no one can be,
the perfect person they want so desperately.
And should my imperfection stop me from loving myself,
or should I continue to pretend to be someone else?
Why would I rather hide in the shell of a perfect girl…
than expose my flaws to this bitter world?
We're all different and that's okay,
for each flower is beautiful,
in its own special way.
Who told us we can't be ourselves,
who allowed us to create someone else?
We crave an unnatural form, to achieve the happiness we look for.
But I'm happiest when I'm me, and not some girl I see on TV.

Anna Vesotsky, Grade 9

Art by Amanda Albright, Grade 12

Mirrors

Mirrors tell you who to be
Mirrors tell you what you are
Mirrors tell you how to change,
When you have nothing to fix at all

We all come in different shapes and sizes,
But yet we all attempt to look the same
But in this world the ones who are unique
And special are laughed at and shamed
I wish people would stop listening
To the hate that swirls around them,
I wish that people would just be themselves,
And not pretend to be like everyone else

Go ahead,
Sit there and stare
At your reflection that seems to have no repair

Mirrors can change who you are,
They force you into somebody else
When you just want to be yourself

It's funny how a piece of glass can change
Everything about someone

I wish that I could do something about it,
But my mirror tells me not to
Julia Barnett, Grade 6

Art by Jing (Olivia) Zhao, Grade 12

Blank Canvas

"Mirror, mirror on the wall, who's the fairest of them all," the one question that all girls face. Every day teenagers are told they have to have waists smaller than the width of their head, long beautiful hair, impeccable skin, and the best clothes that money can buy! Nothing is more taunting to a teenage girl than her own self comparing her looks to other girls. Society today has told women that if they do not look like they walked out of a Victoria Secret magazine they aren't good enough. Media tells us we have to be perfect to achieve our dreams and make it in life.

Recently, I read the book Frankenstein by Mary Shelley. In the story a monster is created from a mismatch of stolen human body parts and chemicals. The world is fascinated by the perfect female body, just like Victor Frankenstein becomes obsessed with the "secret of life." People piece together one girl's hands, with another's arms, and another's chest, and yet another's legs. Eventually you end up with mismatched body parts and the perfect chemical vanity, thus a monster is born, a monster named perfection. However, like Frankenstein's monster, perfection is not real. This creates a problem for most people who, as human beings, seek perfection.

Perfection may be society's look on beautiful, but I see it differently. When I think of beauty, all I see is a blank canvas. A blank canvas is nothing. Who can put one face to gorgeous? Who can tell a woman she isn't beautiful?

Anna Dornan, Grade 9

Art by Kaylie Spencer, Grade 11

25

Mirror, Mirror

Once upon a time there was a beautiful girl.
Each day and every day
She looked into her mirror, mirror on the wall
And each day, every day, she fell into its trap.
She asked this mirror, mirror on the wall,
    "Am I the fairest of them all?"
And that mirror, mirror, full of lies,
    "No, you're not," was its reply.

So this beautiful girl would try, and try, and try
To change that mirror, mirror's reply.
She would change her hair, her clothes, her weight,
But the mirror, mirror's lie always stayed the same.
The harder she tried, the worse she felt.
The mirror, mirror's lies made her confidence melt.
This beautiful girl felt worthless and broken,
Even more so each time mirror, mirror had spoken.

This beautiful girl, she's not alone.
She's not just some random fairy tale told.
She's me, she's you, and the girl over there.
We all have that want, that need to be fair.
But when you look in the mirror, don't believe all the lies.
You're perfect, you're beautiful, just the way that you are.

Tiffany Power, Grade 12

Art by Yang Chen, Grade 11

Mirror Mirror
Sometimes mirrors break
Reflections disappear
But don't let it take away
What you have here

Your heart may feel broken
Like that mirror on the wall
But mend it up with spirit
Keep on standing tall

Turn and look the other way
For it is there you'll find
The things in life that really matter
Are there to fill your mind
Cara Grant and
Payton Hill, Grade 6

Art by Steven Shin, Grade 11

Art by Lisa Anderson, Grade 12

Paper Dolls

She created them
on a gray day
when echoes of cruelty
slithered through her mind
snip, snip, snip
the dolls were perfect
in their bland uniformity
no chance for mockery
of differences.
She saw one doll
that stuck out,
a sharp contrast
to the rest
snip, snip, snip
she trimmed her down
until all truth of identity
was lost for sake
of fitting in
Bryna Sims, Grade 12

The Girl in the Mirror

She looks in the mirror once again, this morning no different than the rest. The same thoughts travel through her mind. The same insecurities are reaffirmed with every glance at this reflection. Not a single feature is thought to be good enough; not a single thought is one of assurance. Why can't I be pretty enough? She imagines herself as someone else, someone prettier; the skinny, long-legged blonde with beautiful eyes and the perfect smile. The girl in the mirror comes back to reality. The immediate comparison between herself and the woman of her imagination is just a deeper plunge into her nonexistent self-esteem.

She continues to school where she sees a thinner girl, a girl with flawless hair, a girl with a better smile, and on and on. All these girls together make up the one in her imagination, but none of them have it all either. She compares her worst feature to another's best throughout the days, weeks, years. She can never stop the comparisons and the negative thoughts, resulting in a rubble of self-confidence. She can never seem to overcome this empty self-worth and realize how truly beautiful she is.

That is just the thing; she is gorgeous! Her hair may not be blonde, but those dark waves are just as ravishing. Her eyes may not be big and blue, but those golden-browns are just as charming. She may not be tall and exceedingly skinny, but that 5'2" girl is healthy and just as lovely. She is just as beautiful, absolutely beautiful! But that is one thing the girl in the mirror has yet to see.

Vanessa Pfeffer, Grade 11

Art by Shiori Mori, Grade 11

33

What I See

They tell you you're beautiful
Don't see how it could be true
Every day just feeling plain and dull
Hating all you see in the reflection
Watching as they walk by —
Only seeing their true perfection
Believing all the magazine lies
Missing the sparkle in your green eyes
The way your smile lightens the room —
You let it go unnoticed
Midst of weeds: a rose in bloom
Hoping that maybe someday —
You'll see what I see every day.

Alison Bloomfield, Grade 11

Art by Corrina Petit, Grade 11

35

Made of Glass

Sometimes it gets lonesome
Going through life,
Living in this skin,
Made of glass.
Never letting anyone in
Fearing you might fall to pieces if you do.
Hiding under a fake smile and fading memories
Of the better life you had.
Forgetting to breathe, crying inside.
But somehow,
You make it.

Whitney Rae Luna, Grade 10

Art by Winnie Ma, Grade 12

Paint Me

I know this being comfortable in your own skin
Is hard
And it always will be
I know this fitting in is a big deal
You want so badly to fit in but think you never will
I know this being an outcast is not easy
You pretend not to be hurt by words but you are
I think we should embrace change
Accepting others should be easy
Because we are not cut from the same fabric
Let's change our ways
We need to accept the weird
We need to change the norm
We need change
I know change is scary
I know I am different
We need each other
We need acceptance…We deserve acceptance
We owe it to ourselves to be more open minded
Paint Me Different Paint Me Open
I am an outcast

Tia Trottier, Grade 11

Art by Julia Stiverson, Grade 12

Skin

Why are you so disappointed in me?
Like I'm not good enough, a disgrace
I tried to be what you wanted, all along
But I found it impossible to be what I wasn't

I managed to cover up myself cleverly
Like a never-changing chameleon
I fooled even myself

I desired those kind lies, useless dreams
A sponge, never quenched
I desired to be perfect, to live under this skin
Yet it began to slowly peel away
Like cheap paint

I saw the real me inside, I liked it

Yet you seemed to dislike this change
Even though I gained more friends
Your confidence in me seemed to fade away

Aren't you proud of me, though?

You begged for "me" to come back
I'm sorry, I can't
I don't want to forget myself again
And this is what I am

Rebecca Xu, Grade 9

Art by Joann Huang, Grade 12

Inside-Out

I wish that I could say
What was on my mind
And not be afraid
Of responses that are made
But my head goes crazy
With things that could go wrong
And then I psych myself out
I guess I'll walk away
I wish you could see me
For who I really am
I know on the outside
I'm as crazy as I can be
But down deep inside
I'm really just scared
So to cover up I joke and I prepare
For the worst to come
But it never does
And then I'm let down
To face it all alone
With no one else to know

Brayden Pinske, Grade 8

Art by Davis Smith, Grade 11

A Mystery Unraveled

She speaks, yet she says nothing
A mystery unraveled beneath her smile
An artwork, like an unsolved case
She's poised; of this there's no denial

Her eyelids plunge in
Dark shadows above her eyes
The grainy texture of her cracked skin
Like a porcelain doll in disguise

Her thin curls bounce off her shoulders
Taking on a life of their own
Her protruding cheeks
Underlined by her caved-in bone

Mountains fade into the distance
Covered by a dark, yellow sky
A beam of light shines onto her face
Never bright enough to show what she hides

Emily Rose Maranville, Grade 10

Art by Yihong Li, Grade 11

Teenagers

It's true you don't know what you have, until you've lost it.
But it's also true, you don't know what you're missing,
    until you've found it.

We walk around like we mean the world,
yet deep inside there's an insecure teenage girl.
We worry about fitting in day and night,
and we want to be different, but we're not sure if that's all right.

We're taught about diversity as little girls,
then it all changes as we become teenagers.
They say girls are made of sugar, spice and everything nice,
but what happens on the days that nothing goes right?

The days we're picked on, the days we're teased,
what if your parents could see you? Would they be pleased?
We aren't all mean but we aren't all nice,
but sadly this is a teenage girl's life.

Bre-Anna Morgan, Grade 8

Art by Yixuan (Judy) Yu, Grade 12

Acceptance

Pressure to be perfect, no chance at being me.
Pressure to be perfect, leave my self-esteem be.

I feel like I am drowning, while they absorb my despair.
I'm left with an empty feeling; and no one seems to care.
What have we done, to deserve their sick, cruel ways?
Why is society so messed up?
What ever happened to the "good old days?"

Pressure to be perfect, no chance at being me.
Pressure to be perfect, leave my self-esteem be.

As I sit and take this in, I begin to see the light.
My heart starts to tell me, "Don't worry, just hold on tight."
And that is my fault for not believing all along,
That I do not need to be anyone but me.
I am myself, and they were all wrong.

"Pressure to be perfect, no chance at being me."

This statement is no longer true. It holds no meaning to me.

I am free. I am finally me.

Erin Gerken, Grade 8

Art by Sebrina Gao, Grade 10

Repetition

Repetition, repetition
Over and over and over again
Like two mirrors facing each other
Looking into one
Is like looking down a long hallway
That never ends
All around me
Repetition
All the people
Look the same
Same hair
And the same clothes
Trying to stand out
While trying to fit in
Fitting in the picture
The blank repetition
Following the leader
The one that no one knows
The one that no one likes
Losing themselves
In the repetition

Ivie van Lent, Grade 11

Art by Amanda Stetz, Grade 11

A Change of Heart

I once had a silly notion
About wanting to be accepted.
I was different from the rest;
I stood out in a crowd;
I wanted to fit in with the rest,
So I became the same as everyone else.
I did that, until someone said this:

"Difference defines who you are.
Difference is what makes you special.
Being different is no big deal
So be yourself
And be happy
With who you are."

I then changed;
I showed who I truly am.
Those who liked me as myself became my friends,
I no longer cared about those who didn't.

I made a vow to stay that way,
And I lived "happily ever after"
From being me, not someone else.

Raymond Wang, Grade 7

Art by Lauren Marin, Grade 12

You

It's tough, I know, fitting in with the crowd,
To feel like you belong, maybe, somehow.

You feel like the world is spinning too fast,
And if you don't get on now,

You might never get this chance back.
So you jump right in,

Hiding your true self,
To feel as if you belong here,

These people, these faces,
All different, they are never the same.

You feel like you have released that tight space

That wonderful, that beautiful secret is out there,
Free for the world to see,

They won't judge, you hope, staring at the floor,
But they do anyway, and that leaves you wanting it more,

What is it?

You know it's true.
All you need here, is to believe in

You.

Claire Kingsbery, Grade 8

Art by Douglas Jones, Grade 12

Her

This isn't me,
This is who I've become.
The real me died a long time ago,
Along with the happiness, joy, and confidence I once had.

I look in the mirror and see a stranger I've convinced myself to like,
Because she's who everyone else likes.

No one likes me,
The real me.

I may not conceal my body in makeup and conservative clothes,
But I still hide myself,
Always suppressing that feeling of freedom that comes when your
true self shines through your eyes like a kaleidoscope of personality.

Maybe I'm afraid, or it may just be habit by now.
You get so used to telling a lie
That you begin to believe it's some miraculous truth yourself.

So I guess the show goes on.
I will continue to play this part,
Because I'd rather people like me as someone I'm not,
than be myself and be alone.

You think you know me,
But you've only met her.

Maybe someday the real me will take off this mask of false identity,
In which a character is plastered that I wake up
Simply to play the role of,
But until then, as a person, I am only skin deep.

Elise Boos, Grade 11

Art by Sue Jin Park, Grade 12

Someone Worth Being
I don't know who I am,
And that makes sense.
After all, I'm only fourteen, a budding human,
Unsure, and just starting to find my place in the world.

So why do people tell me, over and over,
To just be myself,
When I do not even know who that is?
How can I be expected to have found who I truly am,
When it is hidden under layers upon layers of
Expectations and insecurities?

I can't,
And that is why I am afraid.
I am afraid of being myself,
But that is not what scares me the most.

I am afraid that there is no real me,
That I am just the byproduct of the people I imitate.
I am afraid that when I peel away those layers,
I will be nothing at all.

So stop telling me to be myself,
Because I really am trying,
And instead reassure me that there is a person
Underneath it all,
And that I am someone worth being.
Genevieve Claybaugh, Grade 9

Art by Jesse Freas, Grade 11

The Girl in the Pictures

Looking at all the pictures
That seem so long ago
Flipping through the memories
Of the girl nobody knows

So many faces she perfected
But which ones are really hers?
Suffering from things you can't see
Who said time cures?

Broken from being dropped so much
It's no wonder that she cries
Why can no one see
Behind the facade of lies?

Flipping through the picture book
Her face is so composed
Scanning for a moment of happiness
Is the girl nobody knows

Iz Lucero, Grade 10

Art by Euri Chu, Grade 10

61

I'll Prove You Wrong

Don't tell me I'm not good enough,
Because I'll prove you wrong.
The more you say I'm a bad singer,
The louder I'll sing my song.

The more you say my hair isn't long enough,
The shorter I'll cut my hair.
The more you say you hate my style,
The crazier clothes I'll wear.

So yell at me, beat me up,
I'm used to it, immune.
Tell me I'll never achieve my dreams,
It means nothing coming from you.

Because the more you say I am a bad singer,
The louder I sing my song.
So don't tell me I'm not good enough,
Because I will prove you wrong.
Emma Kobb, Grade 8

Art by Amanda Song, Grade 12

63

Freedom: Part #1

The way we see the world, creates the world we see
We portray biased thoughts, and dehumanize our world mentally
We put down our peers, and destroy society with labels
If we just close our mouths and open our eyes,
    this crumbling world would be more stable

Books, television, and magazines they teach women to be perfect
Starvation, anorexia, and bulimia; these controlled girls don't realize
    it isn't worth it
We're so focused on "fitting in" we leave ourselves behind
But what we're leaving isn't body fat or acne, it's our state of mind

We are the blindfolded, thinking we can see
Society can't seem to tell the difference between a dream and reality
We have no idea about what's going on, we are naive
So worried about destruction, peace is something we have
    yet to achieve

We shy away because we are hypnotized by stereotypes
Yet the scars are still there, apparent in the tears we wipe
The media is void of truth
Spawning a path of disaster for our youth

Danielle Gai Simon, Grade 10

Art by Jia Fu, Grade 11

Dear Society

You don't know me, but I know you too well
you think you know how to entice and motivate
but I'm aware of your trapping schemes.
It's tempting to fall into the trends
but I know fitting in never really has a good end.
I don't desire to be "normal"
because I've been called to be different;
don't try to understand, you won't get it.
My values scare those who follow you
it makes them distant;
makes me an outsider, makes me look resistant.
It's not that I have anything against you
but there's no future for society, let's be realistic.
I don't want to be labeled as "go with the flow"
I don't want to become just another teenage statistic.
No hard feelings intended, but it's my choice where I go.

In truth,
a concerned citizen

Shy Neigum, Grade 11

Art by Desiree Counterman, Grade 12

Dear Society

Dear Society,
Oh, what a world you have created,
With your twisted words
And minds

Dear Society,
You tell me to repeat after you
You tell me to look just like you
You tell me to be an emotionless drone
A robot made by you.

Dear Society,
You tell me to be myself,
But when I take off my mask
And hide the mark that you have branded me with
You shoot me down for being me

Dear Society
You put me in handcuffs
And you tell me
That I am Free

Fatima Tariq, Grade 9

Art by Jiwon Shin, Grade 10

Hijab

6th grade.
I made the decision to wear the best and
worst thing that ever happened to me.
"Hijab."
Definition: a scarf worn by women for modesty.
Society's definition of it is a tragedy, I for one call it a beauty.
Making my mind broader and my eyes more open
to the world of politics and deceit.

Heads turning as I walk into a room.
Whispers piercing my ears,
just loud enough so I can hear them. Lifeless.
Laughter silencing and minds awakening.
Looking at me as if I have a bomb in my scarf waiting to explode
and a sign above me labeled "terrorist."

Stares burning into my soul as it paralyzes my heart.
Slowly dying as I see faces turning. Voices yelling in my head,
"I don't know what to do! Help ME!"
But I shake those voices and I walk.
As I sway my loose clothing with pride.
It is a beauty. Getting stares from infants to grownups.
Stares being cut through my skin and into my soul.
Strangling me so I can't breathe, but I pull where there is no room to pull.
I finally got away.
Realizing I might be the same skin color but I am different.
Different, different colors and lengths, she calls it beauty when others say
it's a tragedy to society.
Wrapped around me, called it my serenity.
Killing the venomous words that consumed my every thought.

8 years today, I wear this "hat" on my head like it's a part of me, noticing
nothing but my success. So I forgot the stares and walked into a room of
beauty. 8 years strong with a beautiful tragedy.

Rianne Elsadig, Grade 12

Art by Emily Jung, Grade 8

71

Beautiful

She was beautiful.
But not in the way you'd think.

She doesn't smile in the wake of dawn
And her laugh doesn't ring like a bell.

She wasn't beautiful to many people.
She was quiet and shy and flawed.
And she was perfect.

Her heart was always open
And her mind always wandered.

She would fall in love too easy

And stand right back up.

She was beautiful in a unique, clever way.
A mess of gorgeous chaos
And you could see it in her eyes.

Bayley Peer, Grade 10

Art by Pamela Marino, Grade 9

An Everyday Girl

Crazy but subtle, shy yet outgoing.
She smiles pleasantly, awkwardly sincere.
She walks tall, with her head held high, that is,
    until she sees someone passing by.
She knows who she wishes to be, and sees not who she is.

Her flaws, she is always pointing out,
a long list, too many to count.
High expectations she does hold for herself,
never seeming to reach the goals on the top shelf.

She is an average girl, much less in her own mind.
She wishes to be unique, and strives to be kind.
Little does she know, she is much more than she perceives.
By her own self she is being deceived.

She is unsure of herself, lacking confidence;
    but strives to be poised and optimistic.
She is a girl of the present day, casually fitting in.
And one day, out of the blue, she finds herself in awe.
For she has found a way to be herself, and accepts her every flaw.

Aspen Sierra Rhea, Grade 9

Art by Isabella Taylor, Grade 6

Normal

What is normal anyway?
Average? Standard? The same?
And why is it that being normal is seen as such a great thing?
Do you really want to just blend in
And be exactly like everyone else?
Wouldn't you rather be your own person
And be unique in your own way?
Why would you want to be just like others
Rather than being who you really are?
If everyone would be themselves
Then there really wouldn't be any "normal"
Everyone could live their lives
Without worrying about fitting in
Because no matter what, you know that everyone is different
There is no certain way that you are supposed to be
But no
Instead, people have to spend their time
Pretending to be something they're not
Just to be seen as an average person, not special in any way
You would be so much happier if you would
BE different. BE yourself. BE bold.

Jamie Donovan, Grade 8

Art by Amber Li, Grade 12

Be Different, Be Bold, Be You

Take a look at yourself
Do you like what you see?
Despite all the clothes, and makeup and hair.
Do you see the real person standing right there?
Can't you see the potential glowing within?
What's the point of dimming down?
What's the point of fitting in?
Individuality is the key to freedom
So break out of your cell and start to be someone
Don't be afraid of what others think
Their opinions don't matter so move on with a wink
Life isn't supposed to be serious so have a little fun
Dance in the rain
Bask in the sun
Leave your worries behind and pain at the door
Take a look at yourself because you're worth so much more.

Emma Withrow, Grade 12

Art by Samantha Cheung, Grade10

Flying Solo

Let them live
all mean and mighty,
as a herd of birds,
being all flighty.

I want to be a butterfly,
independent in the high sky.
Graceful and happy by
giving everyone a cheer.

I'd rather be proud and alone
than to follow the herd.
Although standing up for what is right
may put you at risk for a fight.

Fitting in isn't always
the right thing to do.
Fly along and you shall see,
independent is the way to be.

Katelyn Herron, Grade 11

Art by Desiree Counterman, Grade 12

That Is What Sets Me Aside...

"Your past doesn't dictate your future it simply gives you the extra push you need to exceed greatness." I share a story like many African-American females in America, growing up without the one who is supposed to be a provider, a protector, and ultimately a father.

My mother had me at the juvenile age of 16. At such a young age, she dodged negativity, leaped over boundaries, and overcame the odds, all in order to provide a better life for me. Although my story is similar to so many, I am determined not to let my present-day circumstances dictate my destiny. I let my experiences and struggles motivate me to be and do better, and that is what sets me aside.

I yearn to exceed limitations society has tried to set for me. I understand that I am much more than my present-day circumstance; my purpose is far too great, my life far too precious. I am destined for greatness.

I have been taught to reach for the stars, dream big, and believe that I can do anything I set my mind to. I believe that no obstacle is too big for me to conquer because I am not designed to be destroyed. I want to challenge myself with the best of the best. I refuse to be a product of this environment. That is what sets me aside.

I loved who I was, but I adore who I am growing to become.

Trikeria Johnson, Grade 12

Art by Christine Abraham, Grade12

Purpose

Life isn't about being perfect,
a seamless porcelain doll,
on display for all to see.

It isn't about winning,
on the field,
or in the classroom.

It isn't about how popular you are,
or how much money you have in the bank,
or what kinds of clothes you wear on your back.

It isn't about what others think of you,
or what they think,
you're capable of doing.

Life isn't about where you're from,
rich or poor,
because we all have the potential to be great.

Life is about finding your purpose,
finding what you're good at
and what you enjoy.

It's about defying the odds,
breaking down obstacles that get in your way,
and finding what your talents can do for the world.

Keely Lindsey, Grade 12

Art by Trinity Hess, Grade 10

This Is Me

Beauty lies skin deep.

I'm the perfect amount of semi-sweet chocolate chips mixed
    with creamy vanilla ice cream.

People tell me to love the skin I'm in, but in today's world,
    how do I feel beautiful when someone is always
    breathing down my neck.

I shouldn't have to choose whether I'm just White or just African-
    American, so why is it that I can't choose Biracial instead of
    "other?"

What makes the music I listen to "white music" or "black music?"
    The songs I listen to don't depend on the color of my skin.

Why does it matter when it comes to people like me,
    forced into a box of what people assume we are?
    Each of us unique in our own way.

The best part of me is my hair, or so they tell me.
    The science behind these curls mesmerizes people every
    time.

This is all part of the beauty that lies skin deep – from the warm
    color of my skin, to the kind personality that wraps itself
    around me.

I know, despite the labels given to me, I am beautiful.

Amira Hueitt, Grade 12

Art by Vanessa White, Grade12

The Way I See Things

If you could look through my eyes, you would see
The simple good in most everything
And the wonderful place our world can be,
Since people are mostly good, I believe.
Bad things may happen, things may turn out wrong
But don't get lost in the darkness and pain
Learn from suffering, let it make you strong
For there can be no flowers without rain.
So remember the light in your smile
And those that you touch with the love you show
Laugh with your old friends once in a while
And sing along with every song you know.
But what I wish the most for you to do
Is to see all the good I see in you.

Maria Capitano, Grade 11

Art by Ruchi Biswas, Grade 12

My Love

Smile my love
No day can be that bad
Laugh my love
No reason to be sad

Cry my love
No need to hide your tears
Scream my love
Let go of all your fears

Sing my love
With happiness, praises and pain
Dance my love
Through sunshine and the rain

Smile my love
Let your true self show
Laugh my love
Show everyone your glow
Kyla LeAnn Turner, Grade 10

Different

I...
Dance on the ceiling
Sing like no one is watching
Was shaped
To be imperfect,
Noticeable,
Extraordinary,
Unique,
Special,
Remarkable,
Distinctive,
Exceptional,
Notable,
Peculiar,
I was shaped...
To be me
Laurel Smith, Grade 6

Art by Olivia Zhang, Grade 11

Finding Your Dreams
Go for your goals
Reach for the stars
Dive for your dreams
The world could be ours

Make a difference for tomorrow
Cause a change for today
No matter how hard
No matter what they say

Keep hope in yourself
Have faith in all you do
Try your hardest
And always be you

Fight like a champion
Always aspire
Life gives you the keys
Learn to be whom you desire
Sarah Crampton, Grade 8

Art by Allison Du, Grade 10

I Am Me...

I am human, yes I exist, I breathe, I talk and love.
I am me, I have my bad days and I have my good.
I am human, I'm selfish, impatient and I make mistakes.
I am me, I can be weak and I can be strong.
I am human, I can be happy or sad.
I am just a little insecure, and a little wise.
I am young, I am reckless.
I am original and lovable.
I am intelligent, creative and athletic.
I am not an overachiever, nor am I an underachiever.
I am just right.
I can be scared or be fearless,
I can dream, or I can imagine,
I am beautiful.
I am human, therefore, I am me.

Tahnee Drai Shaving, Grade 9

Art by Rebekah Washington, Grade 12

The students featured in this anthology were selected from contest entries sponsored by Creative Communication and Celebrating Art. These students each took the risk on entering a contest and were selected to be published,

To be considered for future collections of art and poetry enter your work at:

WWW.POETICPOWER.COM (Grades K-9)

WWW.CELEBRATINGART.COM (Grades K-12)

About the Editor:

Tom Worthen has been the editor at Creative Communication since 1993. Aside from the yearly anthologies published by Creative Communication and Celebrating Art, Tom was also editor of Broken Hearts Healing: Young Poets Speak Out on Divorce. Broken Hearts Healing received national recognition from Voices of Youth Advocacy (VOYA) and was a Book Sense pick by the independent book stores of America. It has been used by hundreds of school counselors to help youth cope with the feelings created by experiencing a divorce. Tom, known as "Dr. Tom" to his students, teaches at Utah State University where his Speech and Debate teams have won several national championships. He lives with his wife and family in Smithfield, UT.